This Orchard

belongs to

_____

_____

_____

23

For William and Isabel

J.B.

www.johnbutlerart.com

ORCHARD BOOKS
338 Euston Road, London NW1 3BH
Orchard Books Australia
Level 17/207 Kent Street, Sydney, NSW 2000

ISBN 978 1 84616 324 1

First published in 2007 by Orchard Books
First paperback publication 2008

A CIP catalogue record for this book
is available from the British Library.

1 3 5 7 9 10 8 6 4 2

Printed in Singapore

Orchard Books is a division of
Hachette Children's Books, an Hachette Livre UK company.

Can You Growl Like a Bear?

John Butler

ORCHARD BOOKS

With so many
animal noises to do,

Can you make a rumpus

and join in too?

Can you **growl** like a bear,

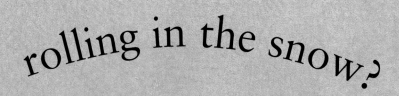

rolling in the snow?

Can you **chatter** like a chimpanzee, swinging to and fro?

Can you **click** like a dolphin, in the wide open seas?

Can you **buzz** like a honeybee, flying on the breeze?

Can you trumpet

like an elephant, on the grassy plain?

Can you **croak** like a tree frog, in the warm monsoon rain?

Can you **roar** like a leopard, slowly slinking by?

Can you **squawk** like a cockatoo, high up in the sky?

Can you **howl**
like a wolf,
in the cool
moonlight?

Can you **snuffle** like a panda, snuggling up for the night?

Everything is quiet now –
you can't hear a peep.

To a hungry shark, the faintest trail of clues is as clear as a restaurant sign.

A shark's nostrils are just under the tip of the snout. Water flows into them as the shark moves forward, bringing any scents with it.

Gel-filled pits in a shark's nose can detect food. Every animal has nerves, which are like cables carrying electrical messages around the body. The shark's gel pits can sense this electricity.

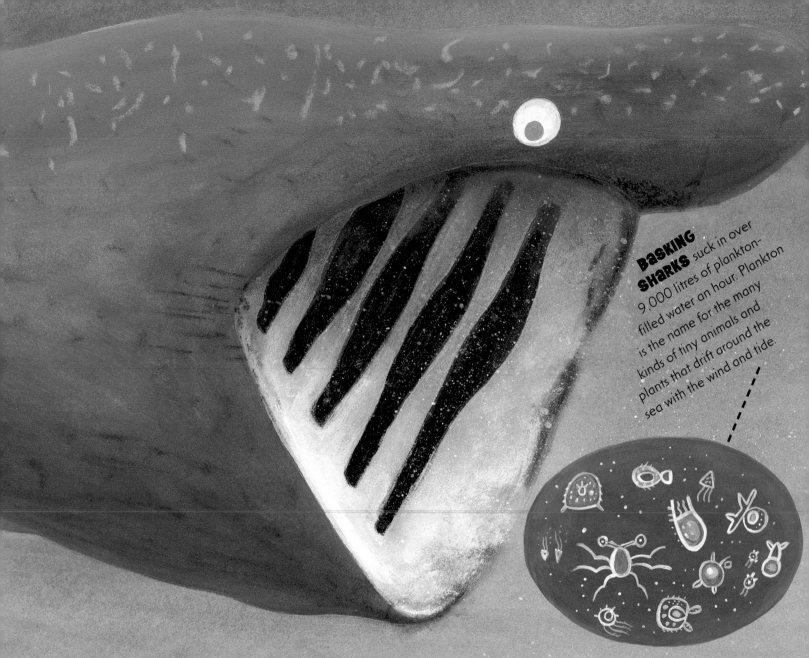

BASKING SHARKS suck in over 9,000 litres of plankton-filled water an hour. Plankton is the name for the many kinds of tiny animals and plants that drift around the sea with the wind and tide.

And when at last they're close enough for the kill, they feel the crackle of their prey's living nerves, so they bite in just the right place ... no matter what the prey! Whether it's plankton ...

or **people**! Oh yes, it's true – some sharks do kill people; about six of us every year.

The **GREAT WHITE** is one of just three species of shark that attack people regularly. The other two are the **BULL SHARK** and the **TIGER SHARK**. In fact, only 30 of the 500 different kinds of shark have ever attacked humans. Crocodiles, elephants, dogs and even pigs kill more people every year than sharks do!

But every year **people** kill 100 million sharks.

Shark-tooth necklace

Machine grease

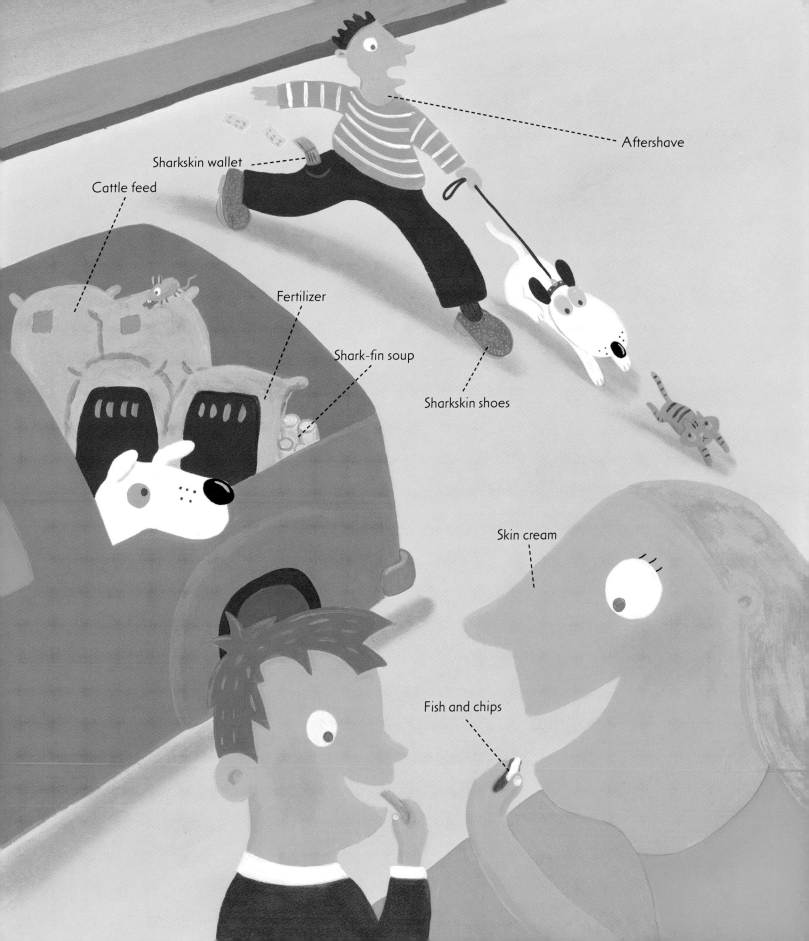

If you were a shark swimming in the lovely blue sea, the last word you'd want to hear would be . . .

hUMaN!

Index

Look up the pages to find out about all these shark things. Don't forget to look at both kinds of words – this kind and this kind.

about Sharks

Sharks have been on earth for 300 million years and can be found today in every ocean and sea in the world. People see sharks as monsters, but of the 500 different kinds of shark in the world, only ten have ever attacked humans and most feed on shellfish and small fishes.

Sharks are predators, they kill only to eat and are as important in the sea as wolves, lions, tigers and bears are on land.

about the Author

Nicola Davies is a zoologist and writer with a special love of the sea. She has seen basking sharks off the Devon coast and once came face to face with a shark whilst snorkelling – a baby spotted dogfish that was the size of a sardine. As sharks have been on earth a lot longer than humans, she feels they deserve our respect and protection.

about the Illustrator

James Croft has always enjoyed drawing sharks. Their teeth, speed and danger have always fuelled his imagination like no other creature.

James lives and works in London.

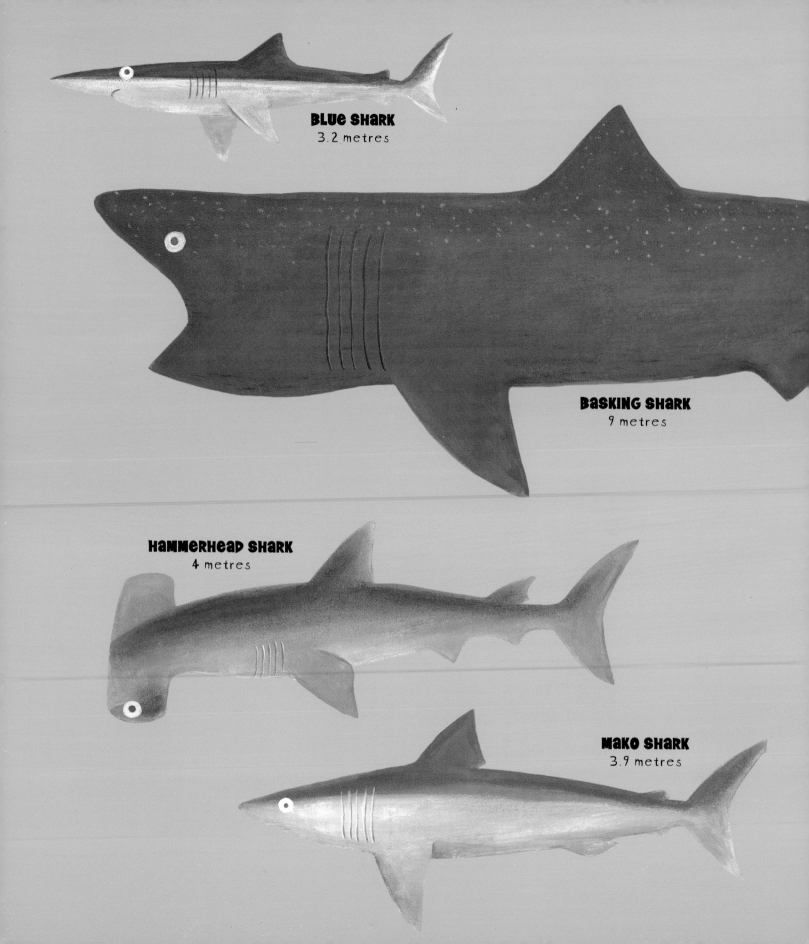

BLUE SHARK
3.2 metres

BASKING SHARK
9 metres

HAMMERHEAD SHARK
4 metres

MAKO SHARK
3.9 metres

Percy bent down and picked one up. There were small tooth marks on it. "Someone's been trying to eat my bulbs!" said Percy. "Who would do that?"

Then, Percy heard something, or some*one*. And the someone was not very happy.

ercy peered out from behind a tree. There was the squirrel. She was digging up another of his bulbs. She sniffed at it and took a bite. Then, she threw it away.

"What on earth are you doing?" said Percy.

"Oh, Percy," said the squirrel in a shaky voice, "I've looked everywhere. I can't find them..."

"There, there," said Percy. "Now tell me, what can't you find?"

"My acorns!" she wailed. "I hid them in a special secret hiding place and now I can't remember where it is!"

"Don't worry," said Percy. "I'll help you collect some more."

"But there aren't any more," she sobbed.

"Well, in that case," said Percy, "we'll just have to go on digging until..."

But before he could finish, Percy was interrupted by a strange rumbling noise.

Suddenly, the mole burst out of the ground in a shower of acorns.

"Oh dear," he blinked. "Lost again. Sorry."
But Percy just laughed.

"It looks like the mole has found somebody's extra special secret hiding place," he chuckled.

"Oh thank you, thank you!" said the squirrel. "Now I'd better hide them again. Somewhere really safe."

"Er...not just yet," said Percy. "Not until you've helped replant my bulbs! Then we'll all go back to my hut for tea and buttered toast. Or perhaps you'd prefer acorns?"

NICK BUTTERWORTH was born in North London
in 1946 and grew up in a sweet shop in Essex. He now lives
in Suffolk with his wife Annette. They have two grown-up
children, Ben and Amanda.

The inspiration for the Percy the Park Keeper books
came from Nick Butterworth's many walks through the
local park with the family dog, Jake. The stories have sold
nearly three million copies and are loved by children all
around the world. Their popularity has led to the making
of a stunning animated television series, now available on
video from HIT Entertainment plc.

Read all the stories about Percy and his animal friends...

then enjoy the Percy activity books.

And don't forget you can now see Percy on video too!